WOOD-HOOPOE Willie

by Virginia Kroll

Illustrated by Katherine Roundtree

Charlesbridge

For my brother, Don, the original Wood-hoopoe Willie. – VK

For my son, Michael Joseph, and my brother, Anthony. – KR

WOOD-HOOPOE (wud hoop´ oh)

Text and illustrations © 1992 by Charlesbridge Publishing
Library of Congress Catalog Card Number 92-74501
ISBN 0-88106-409-2 (trade hardcover)
ISBN 0-88106-410-6 (library reinforced)
Published by Charlesbridge Publishing, 85 Main Street, Watertown, MA 02172 • (617) 926-0329
Printed in Hong Kong.

10 9 8 7 6 5 4 3 2

Once there was a boy named Willie. You could always hear Willie coming. If his toes weren't tapping, his knuckles were rapping.

One day,
Aunt June warned,
"You're gonna jam your
joints that way." Willie thought
maybe Aunt June was just scaring
him into being quiet, but he stopped
knuckle-rapping just in case and started using
some things to help him out instead.

At suppertime, his fork tinkled a tune on his drinking glass
until Mama said, "Stop chiming before you put a chink in that cup."

But Grandpa said, "I'm hearing music."
He thought about *guedras*, drums
made by stretching skins
over mouths of jars,
that he had seen
on his long-ago
trip to Africa.

Once Willie used his knife and borrowed his
brother's besides for tapping on the tabletop. When
he put a slit in the oilcloth, Grandma bellowed,
"Stop be-boppin' your beans around, boy!"
and that ended that . . .

until the next night at Jacobi's Pizzeria when Willie took two hot
pepper containers and shook them so that the dried pepper flakes
clicked softly together.

Mama gave him a dark-eyed stare, and
Grandpa talked about the rattles that the
Bushmen make from caterpillar cocoons,
dried and strung together. Grandpa said
the Bushmen put bits of ostrich
eggshell inside to make that
same soft clicking.

In school the next day, Willie's pencils tick-tick-ticked across the desk top. Mrs. Alston crossed her arms and requested, "William, please wait until music class to display your musical abilities."

But in music class, Ms. White was teaching note reading instead of instruments.

After church one Sunday, when Willie had made rhythms by shaking the change in his pockets, Pastor Nash swished up in his long, black robes.

"Son," he said in a sermonizing tone, "there is a time for making music, but that time is not when I am preaching."

On the way home, Grandpa told Willie about the *ecasas* that the Ga people make by stringing beads over gourds.

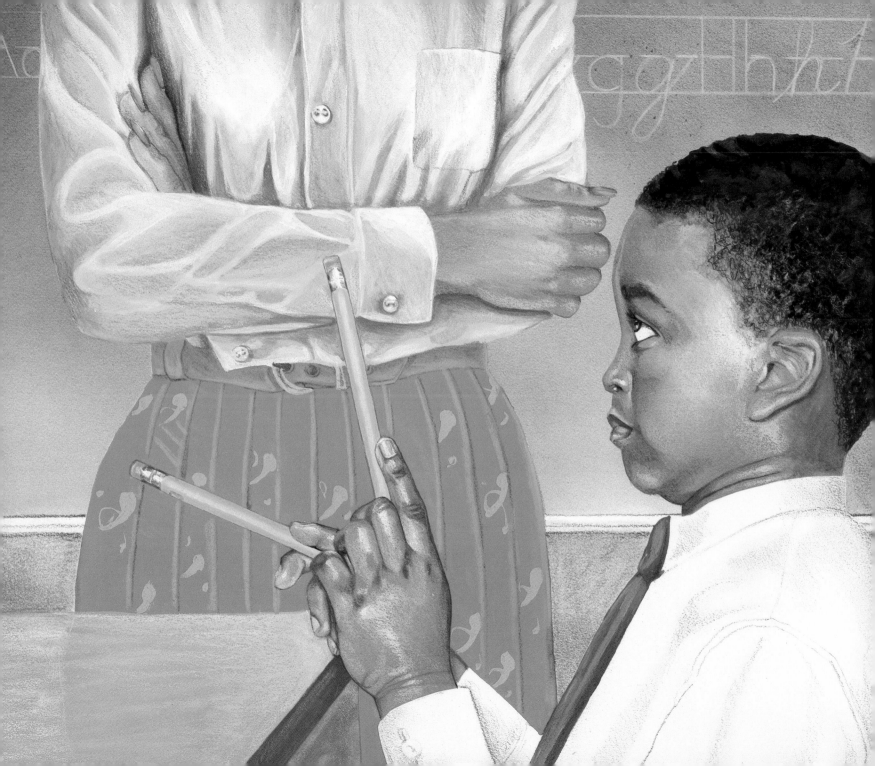

But just to be safe, the next Sabbath day, Willie sat on his hands.

Willie's birthday came. Daddy, Mama, Grandma, Grandpa, Aunt June, Davey, and Willie all went to Kiangs' Chinese Restaurant to celebrate. As they were enjoying their egg foo yung and moo goo gai pan, Willie used his chopsticks for . . . . you guessed it!

Grandma scowled and scolded, "William, that will do!"

Daddy asked, "Have you got a loose switch somewhere, Willie, making your limbs go all out of control?"

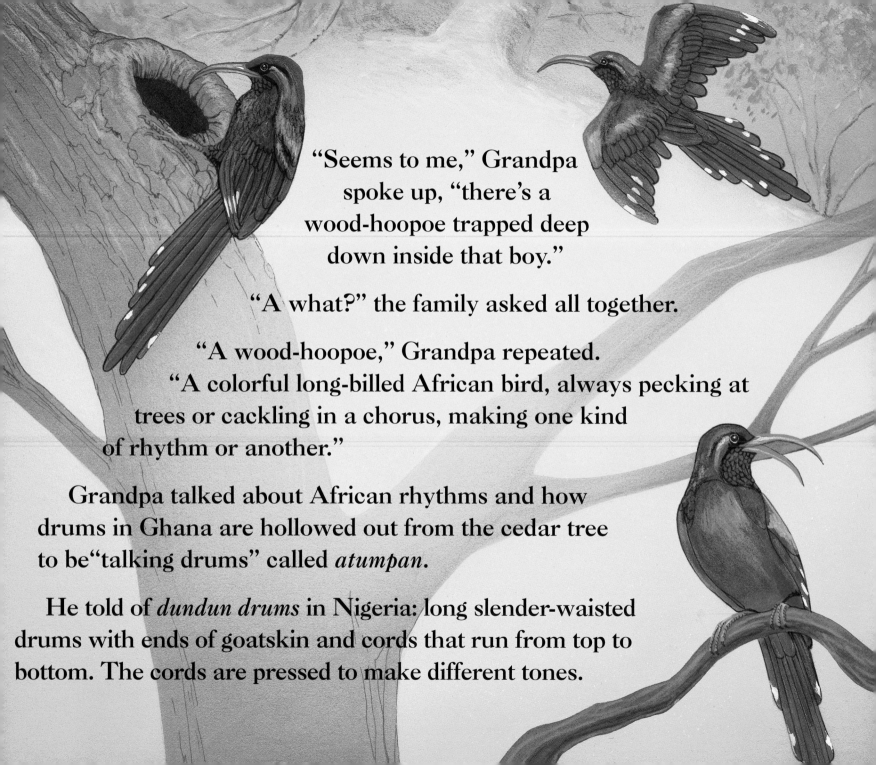

"Seems to me," Grandpa spoke up, "there's a wood-hoopoe trapped deep down inside that boy."

"A what?" the family asked all together.

"A wood-hoopoe," Grandpa repeated. "A colorful long-billed African bird, always pecking at trees or cackling in a chorus, making one kind of rhythm or another."

Grandpa talked about African rhythms and how drums in Ghana are hollowed out from the cedar tree to be "talking drums" called *atumpan*.

He told of *dundun drums* in Nigeria: long slender-waisted drums with ends of goatskin and cords that run from top to bottom. The cords are pressed to make different tones.

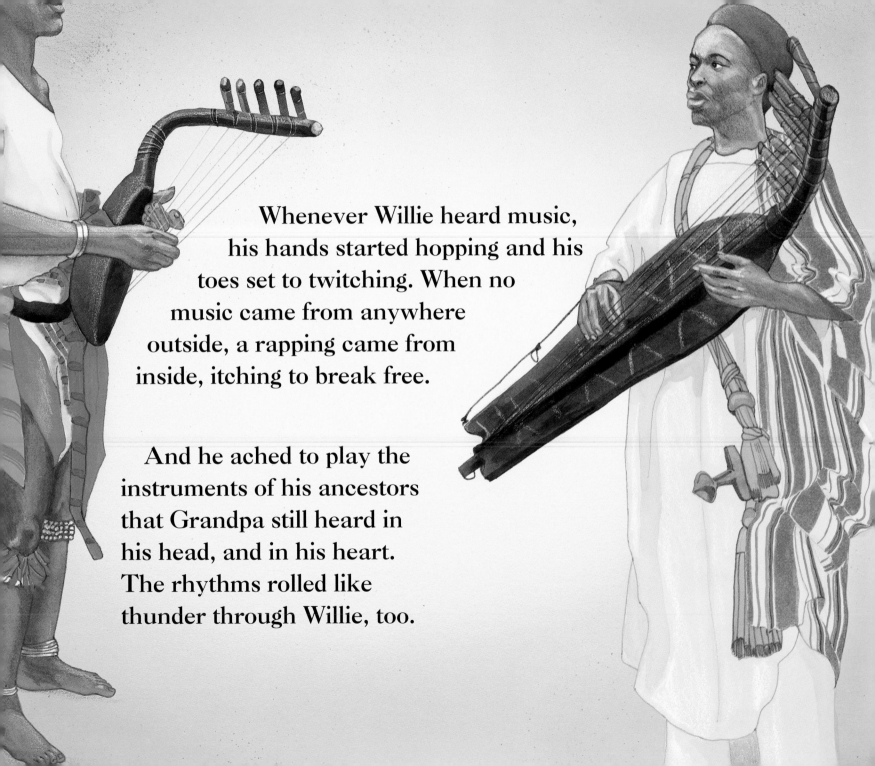

Whenever Willie heard music, his hands started hopping and his toes set to twitching. When no music came from anywhere outside, a rapping came from inside, itching to break free.

And he ached to play the instruments of his ancestors that Grandpa still heard in his head, and in his heart. The rhythms rolled like thunder through Willie, too.

Sometimes at the African-American Center, Willie
watched the musicians. He felt like something would
burst from inside him. And when he went home,
the rappings and tappings were so loud that Willie
got to wondering about that wood-hoopoe.
When winter came, icicles hung long and sharp
from the railings of Willie's apartment building.
One day, on the way to the library, Grandpa
snapped off two thick ones and handed them
to Willie. Willie clinked them together,
and clunked them on light
posts, and rippled
them along the
chain link
fence.

Grandpa told Willie about the melodious sound of *balas* and *balafons*, African xylophones.

One icy, frosty evening in December, Daddy, Mama, Grandma, Grandpa, Aunt June, Davey, and Willie squeezed into the car and drove to the African-American Center for the fifth day of the Kwanzaa celebrations. Tonight they would be celebrating Nia, or Purpose.

Kwanzaa
A family festival

SEVEN DAYS OF KWANZAA

1. Umoja (*oo-mo'-jah*) – unity

2. Kujichagulia (*koo-jee-cha-goo-lee'-ah*) – control of your own life

3. Ujima (*oo-jee'-mah*) – responsibility

4. Ujamaa (*oo-jah'-mah*) – sharing

5. Nia (*nee'-ah*) – having a purpose

6. Kuumba (*koo-um'-bah*) – being creative

7. Imani (*ee-mah'-nee*) – having faith

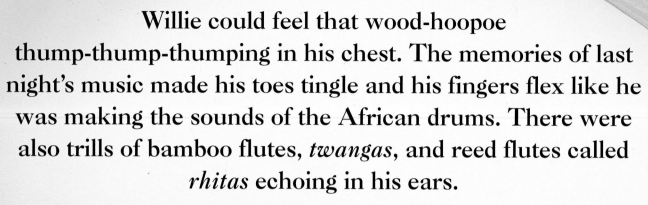

Willie could feel that wood-hoopoe thump-thump-thumping in his chest. The memories of last night's music made his toes tingle and his fingers flex like he was making the sounds of the African drums. There were also trills of bamboo flutes, *twangas*, and reed flutes called *rhitas* echoing in his ears.

Willie and his family parked the car and walked into the Center. Something was wrong. All was too quiet. "Are you sure there's a Kwanzaa celebration tonight?" Willie asked. "There's no music."

They looked
around the Center.
Dancers in butterfly costumes
slouched and slunk. People shuffled
idly about. Women bowed their cloth-wrapped
heads. Men's shoulders sunk, making them look dull
even as they wore their *agbadas*, traditional African shirts.

Suddenly a microphone squeaked and squealed. A man in a zigzag
dashiki tapped on it to make it hush. "I have an announcement," he said. "Our
drummer had a car accident on the way here tonight." The crowd
gasped, but the man held up his hands. "He is OK, but . . ."
He shrugged. "I'm afraid that tonight's
celebration will have to do
without drums."

A loud "aaaw" rippled through the Center like
a giant ocean wave.

"No drums for Kwanzaa?" Mama asked.

"The whole spirit of the night will be lost without them,"
Grandma sighed.

"You got that right." Aunt June shook her head.

"I wanna go home," whined little Davey.

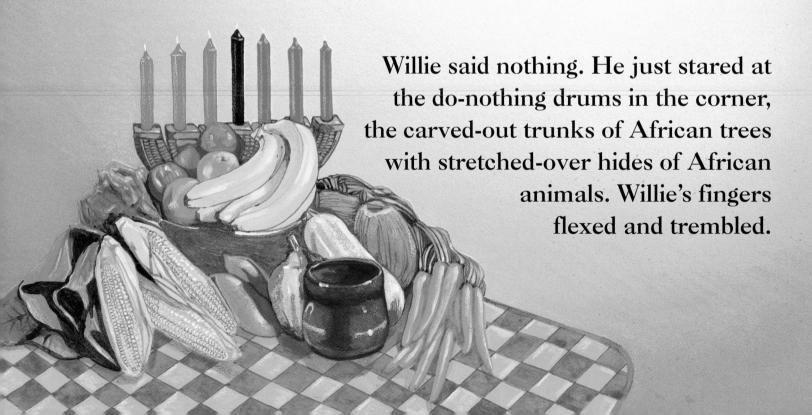

Willie said nothing. He just stared at
the do-nothing drums in the corner,
the carved-out trunks of African trees
with stretched-over hides of African
animals. Willie's fingers
flexed and trembled.

Grandpa crossed his arms and leaned back with a foxy smile. "I'd say it's time to set that wood-hoopoe free," he said.

Willie's stomach did a somersault.

"You waiting for something?" Grandpa said.

Something moved Willie's feet right up to that corner. It made him sit right down in front of the silent hollowed-out trunks. Willie's fingers slid over the skins. They pulsed against his palms.

He started tapping, patting, rapping.
Soon his body was bobbing to the beat.
His heart was throbbing to the thumping.

And his stomach wasn't somersaulting anymore.

The other musicians heard the call and clamored to their instruments. Willie heard the shimmies of the tambourines and the shakes of the gourds with the bamboo stems.

The butterfly dancers took to the air, swooping and swaying, fully unfurled.

Vibrations shivered through the soles of folks' feet and turned their standing into snappy, peppy stepping.

The music drew more people from outdoors. They came in a flock, flapping and clapping, rejoicing in the rhythms, filling up the Center, spilling back out the doors.

Willie looked up. When Grandpa saw him, he made his smiling eyes dart back and forth across the ceiling.

And Willie was sure he saw it, too, zipping and flapping around the room.